COUNT THE SUPERHEROES!

WELCOME TO
COUNT THE SUPERHEROES

GOOD LUCK!

How many superheroes have RED capes?

There are

4

superheroes
with RED
capes!

Count the SUPERHEROES!

There are

SUPER
HEROES!

RED vs GREEN superheroes

There are  **8**  RED
superheroes

& **7** GREEN
superheroes

So there are more RED
superheroes!

How many superheroes **DON'T** have a twin?

There are

5

superheroes
who **DON'T**
have a twin!

How many **superheroes** have orange capes?

There are
4

Superheroes
with ORANGE
capes!

Count the **supermen!**

There are

11

supermen!

YELLOW vs PURPLE superheroes

Which appears the **most**?

There are **7** YELLOW superheroes

& **6** PURPLE superheroes

So there are more YELLOW **superheroes!**

Count the
SUPERHEROES!

There are

13

SUPERHEROES!

How many superheroes are **NOT** wearing capes?

There are

5

Superheroes
NOT wearing
capes!

Super**boys** vs Super**girls**

Which appears the **most**?

There
are **8**

Super**boys**

 & **9**

Supergirls

So there are **more**
Supergirls!

How many superheroes have YELLOW capes?

There are

Superheroes
with
YELLOW
capes!

Count
the
superheroes!

There are

10

superheroes!

Count the **FLYING** superheroes!

There are

FLYING
superheroes!

How many superheroes wear a **mask**?

There are **9** superheroes wearing a **mask!**

BLUE vs PINK superheroes

Which appears the **most**?

There are  8 BLUE superheroes

& 8 PINK superheroes

So there are the **same amount** of superheroes for both!

Count the Superhero twins!

There are

3

pairs of
superhero
twins!

Count the **Super<u>women</u>!**

There are

12

superwomen!

THE END!

BOOKS for little ONES

Find us on Amazon!

Discover all of the titles available in our store; including these below...

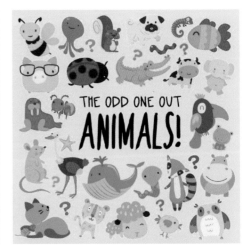

48360598R00023

Printed in Poland
by Amazon Fulfillment
Poland Sp. z o.o., Wrocław